A Suitcase Surprise for Mommy

by **Cat Cora**

pictures by **Joy Allen**

Dial Books for Young Reader

an imprint of Penguin Group (USA) Inc.

DIAL BOOKS FOR YOUNG READERS
A division of Penguin Young Readers Group
Published by The Penguin Group
Penguin Group (USA) Inc., 375 Hudson Street, New York, NY 10014, U.S.A.

Penguin Group (Canada), 90 Eglinton Avenue East, Suite 700, Toronto, Ontario, Canada M4P 2Y3
(a division of Pearson Penguin Canada Inc.)
Penguin Books Ltd, 80 Strand, London WC2R 0RL, England
Penguin Ireland, 25 St. Stephen's Green, Dublin 2, Ireland (a division of Penguin Books Ltd)
Penguin Group (Australia), 250 Camberwell Road, Camberwell, Victoria 3124, Australia
(a division of Pearson Australia Group Pty Ltd)
Penguin Books India Pvt Ltd, 11 Community Centre, Panchsheel Park, New Delhi - 110 017, India
Penguin Group (NZ), 67 Apollo Drive, Rosedale, North Shore 0632, New Zealand (a division of Pearson New Zealand Ltd)
Penguin Books (South Africa) (Pty) Ltd, 24 Sturdee Avenue, Rosebank, Johannesburg 2196, South Africa
Penguin Books Ltd, Registered Offices: 80 Strand, London WC2R 0RL, England

Text set in GosmickSans
Manufactured in China on acid-free paper
1 3 5 7 9 10 8 6 4 2

Library of Congress Cataloging-in-Publication Data
Cora, Cat.
A suitcase surprise for Mommy / by Cat Cora ; pictures by Joy Allen.
p.   cm.
Summary: When Mommy has to travel for work, her son gives her a special picture to ease their temporary separation.
ISBN 978-0-8037-3332-9 (hardcover)
[1. Mothers and sons—Fiction. 2. Separation anxiety—Fiction.] I. Allen, Joy, ill. II. Title.
PZ7.C7962Su 2011   [E]—dc22   2009048974

The paintings were done using gouache and pencil on paper.

To Zoran, Caje, Thatcher, and Nash.
"Everywhere I go, I take you with me."
—C.C.

For Isaac and Luke. Full of surprises!
—J.A.

Zoran was sad because he knew his mommy would be traveling soon. She told him just yesterday morning, "Zoran, my sweet, I have to go to New York for work and I leave in two days."

His mommy always prepared him in advance, but he still did not like it.

"No New York!" he said, and he meant it.

His mommy replied, "I know it's tough on you when I have to go away. I'm unhappy too, because I miss you so much. But I have an idea."

Zoran looked away, because he was not sure anything would help. "Having something special of yours to take with me might make us *both* feel better," she said.

Zoran's eyes lit up and he bolted to his room to search for the perfect thing for his mommy's travels.

The search began in his toy boxes.

Zoran pulled out his favorite truck, but decided it was too big for his mommy's suitcase.

Then he moved to his closet.
He found a robot, but it made too much noise
for his mommy's bag.

Then he went to his bed.

What about my prize pirate? he thought.

No, he would miss it too much.

Zoran could not find the perfect something special for Mommy to take on her travels.

His mommy found him looking upset and asked, "Why is there a cloud over my bright little sunshine?"

He dropped his head and did not say a word.

His mommy glanced around his room and figured it out. She looked into his eyes and said, "Zoran, always remember that no matter how high I fly or how far away I travel, my heart stays here at home with you."

Zoran could not help but crack a smile, and Mommy's words gave him one last idea. He ran to the kitchen and pulled a picture off the refrigerator. "I have it, I have it!" he exclaimed as he ran back into his room.

"The picture I drew for you at school!" he said. It had bright-colored hearts and the words "I love you Mommy" written on it.

"It's one of my favorites, Zoran, and it is the *perfect* something special," his mommy said.

"I can carry it with me right on the airplane," she said.

"And I can show it to my friends at work so they can meet you too."

Zoran piped up, "You could take it to your hotel so when you're in your room, you can see it."

"Yep, I sure can," said his mommy.

"And take it out to eat with you! That's a good plan, Mommy," Zoran said.

"Yes it is," she agreed. "And the best thing is I can put it on my night table when I go to sleep and have a part of you right next to me."

Zoran smiled brightly and jumped up and down. "Yeah Mommy, I did it! I found the perfect something special!"

His mommy laughed and gave him a big hug. "Of course you did, sweetie."

Zoran said, "It's like I'll be with you in New York!"

"It sure is. Gimme five!" she replied.
They slapped hands and *both* felt happy.